Donated

In Memory

Of

MILDRED COOK

by

Harold & Carol Leupp

February 2011

Calvin Coconut

HERO OF HAWAII

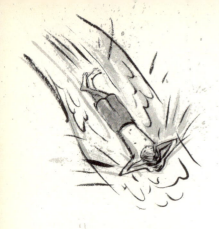

Other Books About Calvin Coconut

Visit us on the Web! www.randomhouse.com/kids
Educators and librarians, for a variety of teaching tools, visit us at
www.randomhouse.com/teachers

Library of Congress Cataloging-in-Publication Data
Salisbury, Graham.
Calvin Coconut : hero of Hawaii / Graham Salisbury ; illustrated by Jacqueline Rogers.—
1st ed.
p. cm.
Summary: When a hurricane causes the river near his Hawaiian home to flood, a boy named Calvin Coconut makes a daring rescue.
ISBN 978-0-385-73962-7 (hc) — ISBN 978-0-385-90796-5 (glb) — ISBN 978-0-375-89795-5 (ebook) [1. Hurricanes–Fiction. 2. Heroes–Fiction. 3. Hawaii–Fiction.] I. Rogers, Jacqueline, ill. II. Title. III. Title: Hero of Hawaii.
PZ7.S15225Cad 2011
[Fic]–dc22
2010013161

Book design by Angela Carlino

Printed in the United States of America

10 9 8 7 6 5 4 3 2 1

First Edition

Calvin Coconut

HERO OF HAWAII

Graham Salisbury

illustrated by
Jacqueline Rogers

WENDY
LAMB
BOOKS

For my Sister, Carol,
a true rescuing angel
—G.S.

For Isabel
—J.R.

1

The Buzz

It was going to be the most famous party our street had ever seen. In two days my sister, Darci, was turning seven, and the buzz was that the whole neighborhood would be showing up, invited or not. The Coconuts were building a slippery slide.

"Ho, man," I mumbled, squinting up at the

sun. "Can it get any hotter?" I'd been trying to think of the perfect birthday present for Darci, something good, something that would really mean something. But it was too hot to think, and I was coming up blank.

Julio humphed. "Where are those clouds when you need them?"

"Or just a breeze," Maya said.

We were sitting on the grass in my front yard: me, my friends Julio Reyes, Willy Wolf, Maya Medeiros, and my black-and-white dog, Streak.

At the bottom of our sloping lawn, a slow-moving river sparkled in the sun. It was the color of rust and almost as wide as half a football field.

Darci and Carlos, Julio's five-year-old brother, were poking around in the swamp grass looking for toads.

Carlos had followed Julio down to my house on a pair of homemade tin can stilts.

I popped up on my elbow. "Hey, anyone want to go swimming in the river?"

Julio made a face. "That stinky water?"

I shrugged.

Maya shook her head. "The bottom is all mucky. Who wants to step in that?"

They were right. It was smelly and mucky. Still, you could cool off in it.

"Looks fine to me," Willy said. He was new to Kailua. His family had just moved to the islands from California.

"Go," Julio said. "Jump in. But don't swallow it."

Willy frowned.

We called it a river, but it really wasn't.

3

It was a drainage canal that carried runoff from the lowlands out to the ocean. I took my skiff out on it all the time, a rowboat that sat in the swamp grass below us. I got Darci to go with me sometimes, but she didn't like being out on the water. She wasn't a good swimmer.

"So when's Ledward coming?" Willy asked.

"Soon."

Mom was still at work, but her boyfriend, Ledward, was coming over to build the slippery slide for Darci's party . . . a *monster* slippery slide that would start with a high ramp at the top of our yard and run all the way down to the river.

Carlos stopped searching for toads and looked up at us. The tin can stilts were slung around his neck, two big cans with strings on them. He took them off and stepped up onto them, then clomped up the slope.

Julio groaned and closed his eyes. His

brothers drove him crazy. He had four, all younger than him.

"Wanna hear a song?" Carlos said, coming over to us.

Willy laughed.

I squinted up at Carlos. "Not really."

"Go ahead, Carlos," Maya said. "You can sing your song to me."

"My mom gave me a nickel, she said go buy a pickle, I did not buy a pickle, I–"

"Come on, Carlos," I pleaded. "Go sing it to the toads."

"–I bought some bubble gum, a-chuka-chuka bubble gum, a-chuka-chuka bubble gum, a-chu–"

I covered my ears. Where was Ledward!

"My mom gave me a dime, she said go buy a–"

"Julio, wake up!" I shouted. "Carlos just wet his pants!"

Julio peeked open an eye.

Carlos stopped singing and looked down.

"Peace at last," I said.

Willy cracked up.

Maya glared at me.

"What?" I said.

"You didn't have to embarrass him."

Carlos's eyes filled with tears.

Maya slapped my arm. "Look what you did."

Julio went back to sleep.

"Hey, hey, hey," I said, sitting up. "Come on, Carlos, I was only joking." Carlos pulled up on the strings that held the tin can stilts to his feet. *"My mom gave me a . . . gave me a . . ."*

He couldn't go on.

"You're such a meany, Calvin." Maya got up and put her arm around Carlos. She kicked Julio's foot. "Don't you care about your brother?"

"What brother?" Julio said, his eyes closed. "I don't have a brother."

I sighed and got up. "Come on, Carlos, I didn't mean it. Look. I was kidding. You didn't wet your pants, and anyway how's about you teach me to walk on those stilts?"

Carlos stared at the grass.

"Come on. I never learned how."

Carlos stepped off the cans and held them up by their strings.

"Cool," I said, taking them.

"Calvin!" someone screeched from the garage.

I glanced over my shoulder.

Stella, holding up the dog-poop shovel.

2

Outstanding

Stella was from Texas and lived with us as Mom's helper. She was in the tenth grade at Kailua High School. She wasn't just bossy, she invented bossy.

"What?" I said, stepping up on the tin can stilts.

"Your mom called and said to clean up the yard for the party."

"So clean it."

"You, Stump. Not me."

I squinted at her. I hated when she called me Stump!

"Justice for the meany," Maya said.

Stella wasn't leaving until I took the shovel. "Let's go!" she snapped. "I don't have all day."

"This is all your fault," I said to Streak.

Streak tilted her head.

"Hey, Carlos, you want to help me?"

Carlos grinned.

"Go on, Carlos," Julio said, his eyes still closed. "I've done it before, and it's really fun!"

Maya grabbed Carlos's shirt. "Oh no you don't. Carlos, don't listen to these fools."

I shrugged. Still on Carlos's tin can stilts, I clomped over to get the shovel.

Stella eyed me. "Are you some kind of a circus freak? Oh, I know, you just needed help getting up to normal height."

She snickered at her own joke.

"So funny I forgot to laugh."

She grinned, holding out the shovel. "Get it all, Stump. We don't need some kid stepping in something."

"Stop calling me Stump!"

"Well, you're short, aren't you?"

"Stop! I mean it!"

"And if I don't?"

I snatched the shovel out of her hand just as Ledward's jeep pulled up. He honked.

"Scoop the poop," Stella cackled, then rode her broom back into the house.

"Darci!" I called. "Ledward's here!"

Julio and Willy scrambled to their feet.

Darci ran up from the river. "Yay! Yay! Yay!"

Ledward got out. He was half Hawaiian, half Filipino, and tall as a telephone pole. He looked down on us. "Is this my construction crew?"

"Yeah!" we all said.

I peeked into the jeep. The lumber was

new. It smelled good. "Can we help you, Ledward?"

"Sure can. You going to work in those boots?"

I looked down at the tin can stilts. "You like them?"

"Used to have a pair myself."

We were as excited as ants in the kitchen. Together we took lumber, blue tarps, stakes, extra garden hose, and Ledward's tool box out onto the grass. Ledward built the takeoff tower

first. It was about six feet high. Then he made a ramp and tacked plastic tarps down over the wood. Below that he staked more tarps into the grass and ran the slide all the way down to the water. But Darci made him shorten it. She didn't want the slide to end in the river, where the current could take you away.

"Ho!" I said. "This is outstanding!"

Later I shoveled up all the dog poop, but I didn't flip it into the bushes like I usually did. I dumped it in the weeds under Stella's bedroom window, which she always left open for fresh air.

By the time Mom got back from work, the slide was done and everyone but Ledward had gone home.

Darci grabbed Mom's hand the second she got out of the car. "Come see! Come see!"

"Wow!" Mom said, hooking her arm in Ledward's. "The kids are going to have so much fun!"

Ledward glanced at the sky. "There might be a problem . . . radio said a storm is coming."

"What's a little rain? They're going to get wet anyway."

"Might be more than just a little rain."

Darci bounced on her toes, as excited as I'd ever seen her. "Nothing can stop my party, nothing, nothing, nothing!"

3

Crumbling Like Sand

The next morning, Saturday, Ledward came back over. He grabbed the morning paper off our driveway and headed into the house.

Darci, Mom, Stella, and I were in the living room, looking out the window at the wild gray clouds. Tomorrow was party day and it wasn't looking good.

Ledward tapped the newspaper headline as he eased the screen door closed behind him. MASSIVE TROPICAL STORM APPROACHES ISLANDS, it said. "Looks like a big one."

Darci crossed her arms. "We're still going to have the party. It's only going to rain, that's all."

Ledward looked out the window and shook his head. "I don't know, Darci girl."

"It does look threatening," Mom said.

Ledward nodded. "Thought I'd come tie down that ramp and get all that tarp up and into the garage. It could get windy."

Darci's careful plans were crumbling like sand in the surf. Two friends had already called saying they couldn't come because their parents were worried.

But the storm wasn't here yet.

Mom hugged Darci close.

"We still have today, Darce," I said. "At least we can do that."

Today Stella and her big scary-looking twelfth-grade boyfriend, Clarence, were taking me and Darci to the Byodo-In Temple as Stella's present to Darci. The temple was Darci's number one favorite place to go. You could feed wild birds right out of your hand, and Darci loved birds. They had a giant gong there, too, which was my favorite part.

Ledward studied the darkening sky. "Better get going soon. My guess is maybe two, three o'clock this thing will hit."

I looked up at him. "But we're still going to have the party . . . right? Sometime?"

Ledward clapped a hand on my shoulder. "Sure! But not this weekend, looks like. Anyways, I should take care of that tarp and go home, stay with my dogs. They get kind of antsy when the wind comes."

Ledward lived up in the jungle. He had a small banana farm, a hairy black pig, and four spooky hunting dogs.

Stella looked disappointed as she gazed out the window. She'd spent a lot of time helping Darci with the invitations, and tomorrow morning she was going to make birthday cupcakes. She had all the stuff ready in the kitchen.

Mom crouched and looked into Darci's eyes. "It looks like we're going to have to postpone your party until next weekend, Darci. I'll call the parents. I'm sorry, sweetie."

"I'll still make the cupcakes," Stella said. "We'll do a practice batch and test them out. It's fun to bake on a rainy day."

Ledward nudged Darci. "Gotta go, but don't worry, I'll still cook for your party, whenever it is. What you like, cow brains or pig guts?"

Stella and Darci made faces at each other. "Eeew!"

Ledward winked. "I'll make some burgers, too."

Lucky for us Ledward was the best barbecue cooker in the world.

He and Mom headed out to stake down the ramp and bring in the tarps.

The slippery slide had been my idea, and

I couldn't wait to try it out. My dad used to come up with ideas, too. Like our last name. He was a singer who gave himself a singer's name: Little Johnny Coconut. He liked it so much he made it legal . . . for the whole family. Now we were *all* Coconuts. It was funny.

For a while.

But Dad lived in Las Vegas now, with a new wife, Marissa.

I pushed that thought away.

A gust of wind rattled the house as Mom and Ledward put the tarps in the garage.

Ledward drove off and Mom came back inside. "Boy, you can really feel the wind picking up!"

"That's how it was back home in Texas," Stella said. "You always knew when bad weather was coming."

Stella's mom was my mom's best friend from high school. She'd married a marine and moved to the mainland, where Stella was born. But now Stella and her mom couldn't get along, so Stella had come to live with us for a while. She was a pain most of the time, but when her boyfriend, Clarence, came over, she almost turned into a nice person. She even pulled out this fake laugh, just for him. Ha-ha-ha, ho-ho-ho.

"Maybe you and Clarence should take the kids to the temple another day, Stella."

"No!" Darci said. "You said we could go, Mom."

"I know, Darci, but—"

Clarence's car pulled up outside.

"He's here!" I said. "Come on, Darce."

Stella grabbed her hooded sweatshirt.

"Oh, all right," Mom said, giving me some money. "Spend this wisely, and you come right home if the weather gets worse, you hear?"

"Don't worry," Stella said. "Who wants to be out in a storm?"

I do! I thought.

Mom looked at me. "You do whatever Stella says, understand?"

"Sure, Mom."

Stella looked at me like, Are you being sarcastic?

"Yep," I said. "I'll do what Clarence says."

4

The First
Fat Raindrop

Clarence played football and worked part-time at the Chevron station. He spoke Pidgin English, like most people in the islands. He had Polynesian tattoos, and drove a pink car with a sound system so loud it loosened your teeth. Two of the speakers were right behind my head in the backseat as we cruised over to Kaneohe.

"Stay out of trouble," Stella said to me and Darci when we got to the Byodo-In Temple. Then she and Clarence went up to the meditation gazebo and pretty much forgot about us.

Which was fine with me.

Clarence had said about zero the whole way over. He was one of those big quiet Hawaiian guys who looked like they wanted to eat you for lunch but were really nice. He didn't try to boss us around or anything.

I banged the big gong a couple of times. Then Darci grabbed my hand. "Come on, Calvin, I want to feed the birds!"

I gave the gong one more whack.

Bong!

Darci pulled me away.

On our way through the temple, we stopped to look up at the giant golden Buddha, big as a three-story house.

"Buddha," I said, looking up at him. "Can you make storms go away so people can have parties?"

Darci grabbed my arm. "Shhh! You're not supposed to talk to him."

"Why not?"

"You're supposed to be quiet."

The Buddha studied me with his peaceful look. I'm happy to see you this morning, Calvin, he seemed to say.

That was what I liked about the big golden

Buddha. He always seemed okay with everything. Like, Don't worry, be happy, life is good.

Darci yanked on my arm. "The birds, Calvin, the birds."

We bought some feed pellets at the temple store and took them out onto a small bridge over the koi pond. It was still early. We had the place to ourselves.

Instantly, a swarm of birds fluttered in to steal the feed out of our hands. But some were shy and you had to toss pellets to them.

A gray-and-white bird with a red head stood on a rail nearby, too wary to jump onto our hands. "What's that one called, Calvin?"

I shrugged. "Got me. All I know is mynah birds, doves, and those all-red ones."

"Cardinals."

"Yeah, those."

I ran out of bird pellets and rubbed the dust off my hands. "Be right back. Need more bird feed."

In the store the perfect present for Darci popped out at me. "Yes," I whispered, grabbing it.

I paid for the feed and the birthday present, which I wrapped up in the bag and stuffed into my cargo shorts pocket.

"Here, birdy," Darci said, tossing a few pellets over to the redheaded one. Then the first fat raindrop slapped down on my arm. Another. Another. A gust of wind whoomped across the koi pond, scattering the birds.

"Ho!" I shouted. "Here it comes!"

The gray sky darkened. Trees staggered and swayed in the wind. A sound roared through them, like a huge truck dumping gravel.

I pumped a fist in the air. "Yee-haw!"

Wild rain bounced off the bridge.

"We have to find Stella and Clarence!" Darci shouted over the roar of the wind and rain.

"Over by the gong!" I shouted back.

We tossed our pellets to the fish and raced

across the bridge into the temple and past the giant golden Buddha, who was still fine with everything. What's your hurry, Calvin? It's just a hurricane.

Stella and Clarence ran down from the gazebo.

"We go!" Clarence shouted.

In the parking lot, Clarence's pink car sat alone. We'd have to run across a long bridge that spanned a jungled gully.

"We'll get soaked!" Darci shouted.

"Ne'mind. Got a towel in the car."

Clarence grabbed Stella's hand, and Stella grabbed Darci's.

A huge tree branch crashed down behind us as we took off across the bridge.

5

Awesome!

"Hoo!" Clarence yelped as we fell into the car and slammed the doors shut. "S'what I call rain!"

Stella's wet hair stuck to her head. She grabbed the towel and tried to dry it, then rubbed Darci's head. The rain thundered down on the roof of the car.

"I love it!" I shook the rain off my head, flinging drops around the car.

"Hey!" Stella said. "Are you a dog?"

Not many things were as exciting as a big rain, and this was *huge*!

We headed back home.

The wind rocked the car at every stoplight. Rain pounded down so loud you had to shout to be heard.

Darci leaned closer to me, stretching her seat belt.

By the time we got down into the valley below Maunawili, the rain was coming down so hard Clarence had to slow the car to a crawl. You couldn't see the road. The wipers were going as fast as they could and still you couldn't see.

"Awesome!" I shouted.

It was like being tumbled around in a

wave, where you didn't know which way was up and which way was down.

Cars pulled over to wait it out.

But Clarence kept crawling ahead. "Not smart to stop here."

I leaned closer to the front seat. "Why?"

"Low land. Could flood."

"Ho," I whispered.

I'd never seen a flood. But I knew what it was. Lots of water making rivers where rivers shouldn't be.

We crept uphill and back down the other side into Kailua.

The streetlights were out. Traffic inched ahead, one car at a time. Fog grew on the insides of the windows. I made a smiley face, then wiped it into a square so I could look out. Everything was blurry.

Lightning blinked in the black sky, followed by huge blasts of thunder that exploded overhead.

"Holy smokes!" I shouted.

Darci gripped my arm.

I leaned closer to Clarence in the front seat. "Have you ever seen it like this before?"

"Nope."

"You really think it will flood?"

"Prob'ly."

I sat back. Cool.

The first thing I checked when we got home was the river. It still looked the same. My skiff sat in the long swamp grass just above the waterline. Probably I should haul it higher up, I thought. My dad gave me that boat just before he and Mom split up. I didn't want to lose it.

We ran from the car to the garage and burst into the house.

Mom was in the kitchen. She looked frazzled. "Thank heaven you're all home safe,"

she said. "I've never seen it rain like this in my entire life!"

I wiped rainwater from my face with my hand. "Mom, we couldn't even see the road. Clarence had to drive slower than you could walk!"

Mom looked at him. "Thank you for driving safely, Clarence."

"No problem."

Stella grabbed his hand. "Let's go find you a dry T-shirt."

"Look in the hall closet," Mom called after them. "There's a box with some of Johnny's old clothes in it."

Mom pushed Darci and me out of the kitchen. "You kids jump into something dry, too!"

"In a minute," I said, and ran to our big living room window. The river sailed past our yard, draining water from the lowlands to the ocean, just a few blocks away.

My skiff was probably filling up with rainwater. I should have left it bottom up.

Mom and Darci joined me.

"The river's getting fatter," I said. "And muddy."

Mom crossed her arms. "I don't like it. I don't like it at all."

6

Rising Water

Darci and I changed and went back into the kitchen.

Mom wanted to know how it was up at Ledward's house. She grabbed the phone, started to punch in his number, and then stopped.

There was a puddle of water on the counter

where we ate breakfast. Mom frowned and looked up at a slow drip plinking down from the ceiling. She handed me the phone. "Here. Call Ledward and see how he's doing while I take care of this puddle."

I punched in his number as she put a cereal bowl under the drip.

The phone rang six times before he picked up.

"Ledward," I said. "It's a storm!"

He laughed. "That it is, boy. How you doing down there? I was just about to call your mama."

"We're good," I said. "Mom wants to know how you're doing."

"Fine. The dogs are howling, but my pig likes it. You got electricity?"

"Yeah."

"Mine's out. Lucky the phone still works. Your mama there?"

"Yeah, sure." I handed the phone to Mom and ran back to the front window to watch the river.

Now stuff was floating in it. The current was picking up, almost like a riptide. I saw a piece of lumber go by, a tree branch, a cardboard box, and some white packing foam.

The wind banged up against the house, shaking it. Trees and bushes swayed and danced around the yard, and the rain was falling sideways. Sharp drops snapped against the window like firecrackers.

A striped beach ball from somebody's backyard sailed across our lawn and bounded down to the river. It made me itchy to get out in the storm. I didn't want to miss any of it.

But who would go with me?

Darci was hiding under her blanket in her bedroom with *Officer Buckle and Gloria,* her favorite book.

Julio?

"Mrs. Coconut," I heard Clarence say from the kitchen. "I can use the phone?"

"Over there by the toaster," Mom said.

"Thanks. Calling home, see if they okay."

I got up and went into the kitchen.

Clarence was wearing one of Dad's old T-shirts. It was too small for him. The bowl on the counter under the drip was filling up. Mom was looking at the ceiling, chewing her thumbnail.

"Hey," Clarence said into the phone. "I Stella's house. You okay there?"

He listened.

The wind outside howled.

"Yeah, good," Clarence said. "I going stay here for now. They live by the canal. It could flood . . . yeah . . . yeah . . . bye." He hung up.

"Everything okay?" Mom asked.

"Can't find our cat, is all."

Mom nodded. "Probably found a nice dry spot to wait it out."

That was when I remembered Streak. I hadn't even thought about her! Where was she? I ran out into the garage. She wasn't in her usual spot by the door.

"Streak," I called. "You here?"

Streak came crawling out from under the car with a smudge of car grease on her head.

I squatted down. She was trembling. "Come," I said, picking her up. "I got a better place for you."

I carried her into my room, which was right there in the garage. When Stella came to live with us and took my old room in the house, I had to move into the storage room. Ledward helped me clean it up and make a bedroom out of it. I liked it.

I set Streak down on my lower bunk and piled my dirty clothes around her to keep her warm. But when I went to the door she jumped off and followed me.

"Don't want to be alone, huh?"

I let her into the kitchen.

Mom looked at Streak and raised her eyebrows.

"Just for the storm, Mom. She's scared."

Clarence waved me over to the window. "You better drag up your boat. The water coming higher."

I looked out to see the river lapping at the stern of my skiff.

7

The Skiff

When I ran outside, the wind nearly blew me off my feet. Raindrops stung as I leaned into the storm and staggered down our sloping yard to the swamp grass at the edge of the river.

Small wooden rowboats are heavy, and even heavier when they're half full of rain-water. The wind had blown my tin can bailer out into the river, so I tried to lift the side of the skiff to let the water pour out.

"I help you!" Clarence shouted.

I dropped the skiff, and the wind blew me off my feet. I tumbled into the boat with a splash and got tangled up in the oars.

Clarence laughed and pulled me out.

"Dang oars," I said, squeezing water from my T-shirt.

Ledward and his dumb ideas. He'd attached cables to the oars so if they fell into the water I could just haul them back in.

Actually, it was a good idea. Except that I usually got tangled up in the cables. It drove me crazy. Last time I'd almost cut them off.

Clarence and I dumped the water out and dragged the skiff up into the yard. We left it upside down with the oars tucked under it.

As we headed back to the house I saw Streak looking at us out the living room window. I picked up my pace. Mom better not see her out of the kitchen!

In the garage, Clarence and I took off our shirts and wrung the water out. Inside, I grabbed Streak and wrapped her in my wet T-shirt to hide her.

I sneaked her past Mom, on the phone in the kitchen, and took her out to my room. I dragged on a dry shirt and went back into the house. This time, Streak stayed in my room.

"I called Ledward again," Mom said, hanging up the phone. "I don't know what to do about this leak."

Mom had put a bigger bowl under the drip. I looked up at the ceiling. It was like a bubble now, and about to pop. "Is he coming down to fix it?"

"It's flooding. He can't get through."

"What do we do?"

Mom shrugged. "Catch water, I guess."

"Can I call Julio?"

"Sure, I'm done. I'm going to get some towels."

Mom left the kitchen as I picked up the phone and called.

"Hey," I said. "What's up at your place?"

"Nothing. My brothers are driving me crazy."

"I bet the river's broken over the sandbar down at the beach. It's halfway up my yard."

"It is?"

"I had to drag my boat higher."

The river usually ended at the beach and never went out into the ocean because the sandbar blocked it. The water just sat there, rusty and warm.

"Hey, you want to go down to the beach?" I said.

"Yeah! But my parents won't like it."

"We can go out your back gate like we're just going to Kalapawai."

"Come on over."

We hung up.

His mom and mine were the same. If we

asked them if we could go to the beach in a storm like this they'd say no. But they might let us go to Kalapawai Market.

I peeked around the corner into the living room.

No one there.

"Mom!" I called. "I'm going to Julio's!"

She answered from down the hall. "Stay inside when you get there!"

"I will!" I said, then whispered, "For a few minutes."

8

Hissing, Roaring, Swirling

Streak was happy in my room, so I left her there until I got back.

The wind and rain were fierce, but Julio lived only a few houses up the street.

I went into his garage and knocked on the kitchen door.

"Hey," Julio said, opening it. "I saw you coming up the street. Kind of wobbly."

"It's the wind! It's awesome!"

Julio looked over his shoulder. "My mom's trying to keep my bozo brothers from tearing down the house."

"Where's your dad?"

"Watching golf."

"Let's go, then."

"Hey, Mom!" he shouted. "I'm going with Calvin to Kalapawai."

No one answered.

"Did she hear you?"

Julio shrugged. "Let's get out of here."

The wind had gotten worse. Trees were bent over so far they looked like they would snap. The noise was wild, hissing, roaring, swirling. Truly, unbelievably awesome.

We staggered toward Kalapawai Market. No cars were parked in front of the store.

"You got any money?" I shouted, struggling to stay on my feet in the wind.

"A quarter!"

"What can we buy?"

"Nothing!"

We skipped Kalapawai and headed down the side road to the beach. When we got to the parking lot at the bend in the road, we saw a cop car. We backed into a hedge.

The wind at the beach was screaming. Words flew away the second you said them.

"What's he doing?" Julio shouted.

"Sitting there."

"We can't go out now. He'll make us go home."

We waited and were just about to give up and go back to Julio's house when the cop car pulled out.

We ran across the park and up a rise to the ironwood trees that lined the beach. We hung on to the trees, looking out at the ocean.

"Ho!" Julio shouted.

The bay, usually a clean turquoise blue, was gray and murky. As far out as I could see, there was nothing but whitecaps. The wind had churned the surface of the sea into high

jagged waves with tops that blew off and flew away in the wind. I felt seasick just looking at it.

"Look!" Julio said, pointing up the beach.

The river had broken over the sandbar and was spewing dirt-brown water out into the bay.

We let go of the trees and raced toward it.

When the wind pushed at my back I ran as fast as a car. When it came back around and hit me in the face I almost had to get down and crawl.

"Yee-haw!" I shouted when we got to the surging river.

Julio grinned.

The river was as fat as I'd ever seen it and

moving like a herd of angry bulls. The sand along its edges was crumbling and falling into the water, the river eating the land away.

Floating junk sailed past and headed out to be lost in the ocean.

The current was so powerful it was like the whole river was racing out and going down some giant drain, only the drain was the ocean. I didn't see any boats out, but there was one crazy windsurfer way down toward the marine air base.

Looking down on the raging river, I could only think: Scary!

Bwoop!

Julio and I turned at the sound.

The cop car, blue light swirling. The cop got out and waved us over.

"Busted!" Julio shouted to me.

The cop refused to let us walk home in that wind. *"Too dangerous!"* he shouted. *"You could get hit by something blowing in the wind!"*

Julio and I slid down in the backseat as we turned onto our street.

"Can you just let us out here?" Julio asked long before we got to his house.

The cop kept going. "You'll get soaked."

"We're soaked already," Julio said.

The cop stopped just before Julio's house. "Fine, but you boys listen; stay inside until this storm is over. Agreed?"

"Yeah," I said. "We won't come out until the sun does."

"Which are your houses?"

We pointed them out.

"That one down at the end is yours?" he asked me.

"Yeah."

"That pink car," he said. "Belongs to Clarence Pavao. Am I right?"

"Uh . . . yeah."

The cop chuckled. "So you folks know him?"

"Well . . . sort of. He's . . . um, dating my . . . my sister." No way I was going to call Stella my babysitter.

Julio looked at me. I ignored him.

The cop smiled. "Clarence is my cousin. Tell him Rudy said howzit."

Me and Julio got out and Rudy the cop drove away.

"That was weird," Julio shouted into the wind.

"Sure was."

"No, I mean, how you called Stella your sister!"

"Would you call her your babysitter?"

"Good point!"

"Laters!"

We headed to our houses.

9

Clarence

The wind wasn't as bad at home as it was coming off the ocean. In fact, it felt like a vacation compared to the beach.

But the rain was still pounding down in buckets. It wasn't possible for me to be any wetter. But the rain was warm, and that was good.

Streak barked. She was looking out my bedroom window, her nose pushing at the screen.

"Hey, girl!" I shouted.

I went into the garage and let her out. I took my shirt and shorts off, wrung them out, and got dry ones off the floor.

Streak followed me into the kitchen.

Clarence was emptying the bowl under the leak.

"Hey," he said. "Where you went?"

"Where's everyone?"

"Had to get groceries. Candles, too, case you lose power."

"They went shopping in a storm?"

I peeked back out into the garage. Mom's car was gone and I hadn't even noticed.

"Watching the leak while they gone," Clarence said.

Huh. Felt kind of weird to be home alone with someone I hardly knew.

Clarence must have noticed. He chuckled.

"They be back soon. So . . . where you went? Just curious."

"Me and Julio, we went down to the beach to see if the river was going into the ocean."

"Gotta be, ah?"

"Like a freight train."

"Take you right out to sea," Clarence said.

That was a scary thought.

"You check your boat?" he said.

"No."

Clarence set the empty bowl under the drip. "We go. That river coming higher by the minute."

We stood just inside the garage looking out. Raindrops splashed up over my feet and legs. The river was almost up to my skiff again, climbing the slope of our yard.

"How high do you think it will get?" I asked. "Could it reach our house?"

"Well, you pretty high up."

Through the wall of rain I could make out the rickety old wooden golf course bridge that spanned the water just upriver. I'd fished off it lots of times. There was a small platform out near the middle where you could sit. A few more feet and that platform would be under water.

"Let's get your boat."

We pulled the boat up to the top of the yard and left it bottom up. Back in the garage, we took off our soaked shirts and squeezed them out.

"Listen," Clarence said. "I gotta go home. Watch that leak . . . and tell Stella I said bye, ah?"

"Yeah, sure . . . you coming back?"

"Tomorrow. Right now I got to make sure my moms and sister doing okay."

"What about your dad?"

Clarence snorted. "No more dad. Like you, ah?"

"I have a dad."

"Yeah?"

"He's a singer. He lives in Las Vegas."

Clarence nodded. "That's good, then."

"Yeah."

He started for his car.

"Wait," I said. "Your cousin Rudy said hi."

Clarence stopped. "How you know Rudy?"

"Uh . . ."

Clarence grinned. "Ah, the beach, right? He made you come home."

I frowned.

"Hey, no worries. I won't tell."

He was okay, Clarence.

"Watch the river," he yelled as he got into his car. "It starts coming up too high, call me. We make some sandbags for the house."

Sandbags?

I looked at the river.

The rain roared on.

10

Bug Explosion

When Stella, Mom, and Darci got home from the store, I said, "Clarence went to check on his mom and sister."

Mom plopped a droopy wet grocery bag on the counter. "Shopping in a storm is no fun."

"He said to say bye," I added.

Mom started taking things out of the bag.

"What's Clarence's family like, Stella? They obviously raised him well."

"Nice. They live in a little house on the other side of the river. His dad and uncle live there, too."

"What?" I said. "He said he didn't have a dad."

"Well, actually the dad is Lovey's, not his."

"Lovey?"

"His sister, pea brain. You should know her. She goes to your school."

"Lovey Martino?"

Stella snapped her finger and pointed at me. "Bingo."

"But Clarence's last name isn't Martino," I said.

Stella gave me a sad look. "Your lightbulb isn't very bright, is it?"

"Stella," Mom said.

"Fine. She's his half sister. Different dad."

Ho! Lovey Martino was Clarence's *sister*? Man, was Tito going to be surprised about that. Tito'd met up with Clarence once and was scared of him. Tito was this sixth grader who always bothered us at school. He followed Lovey Martino around like a shadow, even though Lovey wouldn't give him a crumb off her lunch plate. Tito also liked Stella, who thought he was an idiot.

Mom looked at me as she put stuff away. "How's everything at Julio's house, Cal?"

"Oh . . . good."

"Do they have any leaks?"

"Uh . . . no," I said, hoping that was true. I made myself busy by emptying the leak bowl and setting it back under the drip.

Plink.

The phone rang.

Stella answered cheerfully, hoping, I guess, that it was Clarence. "Hello-o."

I started for the door before Mom could ask any more questions.

"Hey, twit!" Stella called. "It's Willy."

I took the phone. "Hey, Willy."

Stella and Mom left the kitchen.

"Can you believe this storm?" Willy said.

"No kidding. You should see the river. It's rising."

"Is it going to reach your house?"

"I sure hope not."

We were quiet a second.

"Hey," I said. "You want to sleep over tonight? Ask your mom."

"Yeah, great. Hang on."

I held my hand over the phone. "Mom," I called. "Can Willy sleep over?"

"If it's okay with his mother it's okay with me," she answered from the living room.

Willy came back. "She said I could."

"Cool. Come now. Bring your sleeping bag. My other bunk doesn't have sheets on it."

"Be right there." Willy lived down the street, a few houses past Julio's. We hung up.

A half hour later Willy came dripping in through the garage and stuck his head into my room. "You in here?"

"What took you so long?"

Willy tossed his sleeping bag on the lower bunk. "I had to clean my room first. Hey, Streak."

Streak lay on a small rug on the polished concrete floor. She thumped her tail.

"Cleaning your room sounds like bribery to me," I said.

"Totally."

It was getting darker outside. "Let's go see what's for dinner."

It was almost like camping out. Mom and Stella cooked up hot dogs and beans and sliced some apples. Willy and I took our plates out on the covered patio and sat watching the rain pour off the roof so hard it dug trenches in the sandy soil below. It was loud, too.

Willy shouted, *"Hot dang! Can you believe this rain?"*

"Double dang! Ho!"

He grinned.

Back in my room it was just as noisy. Rain was misting through my screen, but only onto the windowsill.

Something else was coming into my room, too.

"*Yai!*" Willy yelped, and scrambled up onto the top bunk. "Look on your desk! It's Manly Stanley!"

Manly Stanley was our class pet, a centipede that I'd caught in a jar and that now lived in a sandy resort on our teacher's desk at school.

"That's not Manly, it's his uncle, Legs. Hey, Legs," I said to the centipede. "Where you been?"

My desk was a counter that ran along one side of the room. Behind it was a stone wall, which was the old garage wall before someone who lived here before us made a storage room out of half the garage. There were cracks in the rock. That was how bugs of every kind got in.

"They come in when it rains. Kind of like a bug explosion."

"Great."

I laughed. The centipede was pretty big, about four inches. It would probably look like an alien from outer space through a microscope. "Don't worry. The small green-head ones are worse."

"I feel better already."

"Those ones you don't see until they bite."

Willy looked down from the top bunk. "Can't you get it out?"

"Sure . . . but there'd just be more of them."

Willy's mouth hung open. "We gotta sleep with those things in here?"

"They won't bite you. They just want to be dry, is all."

Willy frowned. "Fine, but I'm not sleeping on the bottom bunk."

We traded beds. I handed him his sleeping bag and he tossed me my pillow and sheet.

I snapped my fingers. Streak jumped up on my bed and plopped down by my feet.

"Say good night to Spidey," I said to Willy.

"Who's Spidey?"

"Look in the corner above your head."

"Aw, man!"

"He won't bite, either."

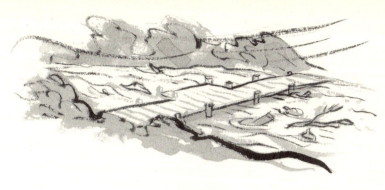

11

The Bridge

It was still raining when I woke up the next day, Sunday. My window was filled with dark gray clouds and the sound of endless rain. It was supposed to be Darci's party day, but that would have been a disaster in this weather.

I got up on my elbows.

My blinking clock said it was 2:18. The

power had gone out and come back on in the night.

"Willy," I whispered. "You awake?"

No answer.

Streak stretched and yawned, sleeping by my feet.

I peeked up over the top bunk. Willy wasn't there.

I pulled on yesterday's shorts and T-shirt, and Streak and I headed to the kitchen. The smell of bacon hit me like a brand-new sunny day.

A glass bowl of pancake batter and a carton of eggs sat ready by the stove. Willy and Darci were sitting at the counter near the leak bowl with glasses of orange juice.

Mom looked at me from the stove, a spatula in her hand. "Good morning, sleepyhead."

"What time is it?"

"Almost nine-thirty."

"It's still raining." I was getting worried, because it had never rained so hard for so long.

"It's supposed to let up sometime this

morning. At least, that's what Ledward said. He called. Still stuck."

"My boat!" I ran to the living room to look out the window. Willy jumped off his stool and followed.

"Come right back," Mom said. "I'm starting the pancakes and eggs."

The river was as wide and high as I'd ever seen it in my whole entire life, so high it made my stomach swirl. Scary! My skiff was still above it, but not for long. I hoped Ledward was right about the rain ending soon.

"Look at the bridge!" I said.

The water was nearly to the top. There was only about six inches left to go and—boom— that bridge would be under water.

"I hope the river doesn't take it out," Willy said.

"Prob'ly could, too."

We ran back into the kitchen. While we ate the best breakfast ever—bacon, eggs, and pancakes taste so good in the middle of a storm— the rain started to let up.

"Finally," Mom said.

Stella came into the kitchen. She looked at me and Willy. "Hurry up. I need the kitchen."

"For what?" I asked.

"For this," she said, holding up a fist.

"Stella's making cupcakes," Mom said. "Special ones for Darci."

I scrunched up my face. "What's special about cupcakes?"

Stella moved up next to me, so close I could smell her toothpaste. She put her arm around me. "So, Stumpy, listen. If you saw a special cupcake would you even know it was special?"

I shrank away from her arm.

Willy gaped.

"The answer is no," Stella said. "So I ask myself: Why are we having this conversation?"

Mom pointed out the window. "Look! The rain stopped."

My ears swelled in the sudden silence.

Now there was only the rattle of the wind slapping at the window screens.

I shoved Stella away and gobbled down what was left on my plate.

"Let's get out of here," I said to Willy.

"Wait, wait, wait," Mom said. "Where are you going?"

"Just outside, Mom. Check stuff out."

"Okay, but you listen to me—don't get close to that river! It's moving very fast."

"We won't." We headed for the door.

"Let's go check out the bridge," I said to Willy.

Streak was in the garage. She hopped up when she saw us.

"Stay," I commanded. "Guard the house."

I didn't want her falling off the bridge or something.

Streak was getting better at staying when I said to.

Willy and I blasted out into the dark gray day.

The wind wasn't nearly as powerful as it had been the day before, but it was still strong.

We ran across the street, through the jungle, and out onto the golf course on the other side. There was no way any golfers would be out on this day.

Long swamp grass along the shore bent in the wind. On sunny days we found lost golf balls in it and sold them back to golfers for a quarter.

The bridge looked the same as always. But the river was very close to having it for a snack.

I grabbed Willy's arm and held him back. "Too spooky to go out there."

"Looks okay to me."

He started out.

I frowned. "Go slow, then," I said, creeping along behind him. "Better not go at all."

"It's fine. Look. It's solid. Not rocking or anything."

The water raced under it, a gazillion gallons, all muddy brown and littered with floating junk. The river moved so fast it made the bridge hum. I could feel the vibrations in my feet and legs.

We walked out to the small platform, taking careful steps, ready to run back if the bridge started to feel weird.

So far, so good.

We crept out onto the platform and crouched. The swirling water made me dizzy.

Downriver I could see my house with my skiff high up in the yard. Farther toward the ocean, the road bridge that crossed over into Lanikai only had a small space under it, too, but it sat higher than the one we were on, and it was way stronger.

"Man, look at all the junk in the water," Willy said.

Branches from the mangroves that lined the river had broken off and were sailing downstream. Some got caught under the bridge.

"Here comes a big one," I said.

It was mostly submerged, but parts of it stuck out of the water. It was heading right toward us and would go under the platform if it stayed on course. Willy crawled to the edge

and looked into the water. "Let's watch it go by."

I got down next to him. The branch flowed under, and when it popped out on the other side Willy reached down and grabbed it.

I blinked and he was gone. The branch had pulled him off the platform into the muddy water.

"Willy!"

He looked back at me as the river swept him away.

12

Tangled Oars

*"**Willy!**"* I screamed again.

He was still hanging on to the branch as it dragged him toward the sea. He bobbed, then went under.

I gasped.

He popped back up.

A huge gust of wind rattled the bridge. I

jumped up and leaned into it, started running. Back to the fairway. Along the swamp-grass shore. Into the jungle, pounding down the trail. I broke out onto the street across from my house.

The street was deserted.

Nothing but the wind and empty yards.

Off to my right the river sailed on, and I could see Willy, still clinging to the branch. In a minute he'd glide past my yard. I ran down to the waterline, now eating up most of our yard.

"Willy!"

He couldn't hear, too busy struggling to hang on to the branch, trying to keep his head up.

"Swim to shore!" I shouted. *"Let go and swim!"*

Willy was new here. He didn't know about getting out of currents. I'd never even seen him swim. Did he know how?

The boat!

I ran to my skiff, flipped it over, and dragged it toward the water. The oars fell out, twisting in their cables, flopping around behind.

Glancing up at the house, I saw Darci watching me in the big front window.

"Willy's in the water!" I yelled. *"Get Mom!"*

But Darci couldn't hear me. She disappeared from the window.

Willy was even with the yard now. There was no way he could angle in to shore before he passed. He was too far out and moving too fast. I'd have to get the boat out and catch up, grab him before the current dragged him out into the ocean.

A car pulled up.

Clarence!

He saw me untangling the oars and ran

down to me, leaving his car door open. "You
can't go out on that water!"

"Willy fell in the river!"

"Where?"

"That branch! See him?"

I tried to unhook the cables from the
oarlocks but couldn't. *Why did Ledward do this!*

"Wait!" Clarence said. "I going the house,
tell them. Stay here. We go together!"

Clarence sprinted toward the door.

I got the oars untangled and tossed them into the skiff.

Willy hadn't said a word since he'd fallen in. No screams, no yells. Just silence. Scary, scary silence.

He was past the yard now, moving toward the second bridge.

And the ocean!

No time. I shoved the skiff out and jumped in.

"Hey!" Clarence yelled behind me.

I turned to look back. Clarence held his head in his hands. Streak ran from the garage, down to the water. She barked at me.

Mom ran out.

She shouted something, her words muffled by the wind.

Streak barked and barked as the current grabbed the boat. I fumbled with the oars.

Ahead, Willy still clung to the branch. Moving closer to the bridge. Closer, closer.

Three feet separated the bottom of the bridge from the surface of the river. Willy was low in the water. He could make it under.

But could I?

13
Wall of Water

The closer the river got to the ocean, the faster it ran.

The wind howled in my ears, but the muddy water was eerily silent. I could see Streak running along the shore.

Just as the skiff reached the bridge, I dove

onto the floorboards, flattening myself to make it under. The oars fell into the water. The current spun the skiff around, the stern thunking one of the bridge pylons.

I popped up on the other side.

Willy bobbed ahead of me.

"Willy!" I called.

He looked back, still clinging to the branch.

"Hang on! I'm coming!"

I grabbed the cables and dragged the oars into the boat. The skiff spun. I got the oars into the oarlocks and tried to turn the skiff around and head straight out so I wouldn't cross the sandbar sideways and flip over.

Three boys onshore spotted us and ran through the trees at the top of the sandy rise. Streak ran with them.

I tried to row, but the skiff kept spinning in the current.

Right where the river emptied into the ocean, the water sank into itself, then rolled back up and over in a wild mud-water wall.

Willy hit it head-on. It sucked him under. Pieces of the branch he was hanging on to shot up above the surface, then vanished.

The boys onshore jumped up and down, yelling, pointing.

I dug my right oar in to turn the boat. If I hit that wall sideways it would tip me over and I'd get sucked under like Willy.

The skiff turned just as I hit it.

Boom!

I let go of the oars and grabbed the sides of the boat, hanging on as the skiff shot into the air. It came smashing down on the other side, swirling in the foamy confusion.

But I was still in it!

I dragged the oars into the skiff. *"Willy! Where are you?"*

Nowhere.

I caught a glimpse of Clarence and Stella racing down onto the beach.

I started rowing, looking for Willy. I gave it all the muscle I had, but the raging current sucked the skiff out toward Flat Island, a pancake-shaped piece of land, the only solid ground between the beach and a few thousand miles of open ocean.

Onshore, I saw Streak race into the waves.

"No!" I shouted. "Streak, stay!"

"Calvin!"

I whipped around.

Willy!

He raised a hand. "Help!"

He was behind me, just beyond the swirling wall of the muddy river. I squinted, my eyes stung by the wind that spat needles of white water off the sea. Willy'd lost the branch.

He sank, came back up.

And went under again.

14

Overboard

"**I**'m coming! I'm coming!"

I struggled to keep the oars in the oarlocks, then put my back into it, trying to dig deep and pull with all my strength. When you row, you sit backwards. You can't see what's in front of you. I had to keep looking over my shoulder.

Find Willy!

The wild whitecaps slammed me around, waves banging the hull.

Somehow I got the skiff headed back toward Willy, and now Streak, who was swimming into a mess she might not survive.

On the beach, Clarence ripped off his shirt. It was crazy, but he was coming in. I hoped he was a strong swimmer. We were a long way out.

"*Cal—*" Willy called.

One second I could see him, the next he was lost in the chop. But he was struggling to swim to me.

The muscles in my arms burned. I was barely managing to keep the skiff from blowing out to sea.

Inch by inch, we closed the gap.

When I got close enough I stopped rowing.

Willy was losing it; his arms barely made it out of the water. "*Just a little more, Willy!*" I knelt and reached over the side.

But the wind pushed the skiff away.

I sat back and rowed again, looking over my shoulder.

"*Stay up! Willy, stay up!*"

I threw down the oars and hung over the side, reaching out.

Willy looked at me . . . and sank.

"*No!*"

I jumped overboard and dove down. I

grabbed him and dragged him to the surface. He gasped and clawed at me, pulling me down.

"No, Willy! Don't!"

But he was desperate.

I went under and he let go.

I came back up and grabbed him from behind. "I got you, Willy, I got you!"

The wind had taken the skiff away from us. Too far to reach.

My arm banged something hard.

An oar!

I grabbed it and hung on with one hand, my other hand gripping Willy's T-shirt.

"*Okay, listen. I'm going to let you go. Hang on to my back!*" I shouted.

Willy nodded and grabbed my shoulders.

With both hands, I pulled us toward the skiff by the cable attached to the oar. I gripped the stern and hung in the water a second, breathing hard. Willy let go and tried to pull himself aboard. But the skiff tipped toward him, taking on water.

"*Willy, no!*"

But Willy wouldn't let go.

I pulled him away, but the skiff was half sunk. It was still floating, but all we could do now was hang on and wait for help.

I couldn't see Streak in the chop.

Or Clarence.

If I couldn't see him, would he see us?

15

Hero of Hawaii

Willy and I hung on as the wind and the current took us farther out to sea.

We were closing in on Flat Island, but it was so small we would miss it unless we could somehow break free from the current and change course. With a half-sunk boat that we couldn't even get into, that would be almost impossible without help.

Flat Island was close enough to swim to. But did Willy have the strength to try?

I turned back toward the beach. I saw Mom and Darci, other people, Willy's parents, and two police cars.

"Willy!" I shouted. "You doing okay?"

He nodded.

Then I remembered Streak!

I kicked to get higher in the water. *"Streak!"*

She was close, bobbing in the chop, swimming toward us. She looked like a wet rat.

Past Streak, I caught a glimpse of Clarence. His stroke looked strong.

"Over here!" I called.

Streak finally made it.

I got hold of her and wrestled her up. She scrabbled into the half-sunk skiff.

Clarence swam hard the last few yards. "You two all right?"

"Yeah." I gulped a breath. "But Willy . . . almost drowned."

"I'm . . . so . . . tired," Willy mumbled.

Clarence looked into the skiff, then back at the beach. He waved to the people onshore, gave them a thumbs-up.

"Listen," he said. "We going put your friend inside with the dog, then we pull the boat to that small island. Can you do that? You still strong?"

"Think so."

"We go."

Together, Clarence and I pushed Willy up into the skiff.

Clarence got the oar that was in the boat. "Grab the other one! We pull." With all the water in the skiff, we might as well have been trying to pull a container barge. But it was the only way.

We turned on our backs, gripped the oar cables, and kicked toward Flat Island.

Inch by inch.

Straining, pulling.

Muscles burning.

We pulled into a small cove and dragged the boat up onto a coral beach. Streak ran up onto the island. It was flat, like its name, about five feet above the water.

We helped Willy out of the skiff. His teeth were chattering.

Clarence nodded toward a sheltered spot out of the wind. "Put him over there."

Willy sat with his knees up, his arms and head resting on them.

"Stay with him," Clarence said. "Try to warm him up. I get the water out of that boat."

He dragged the skiff higher up and tipped the water out.

I rubbed Willy's arms. His lips were blue. I wondered if the golden Buddha would say *Don't worry, be happy* now. Prob'ly.

Streak came back and leaned up against me, trembling.

"You crazy dog. You swam out to save me, didn't you?"

She licked my face.

Clarence came back to help me rub Willy warm.

"Was brave, what you did," Clarence said to me.

I stared at Willy's pale face, his blue lips. It wasn't brave, it was terrifying. Willy could have drowned.

"Very, very dangerous, this kind of water," Clarence said, working on Willy's legs. "The current, undertow, sharp stuff floating in the water. Hard to swim. Get tired fast. Easy to drown." He lifted his chin toward Willy. "But you did um anyway."

"So did you."

Clarence put his hand on my head and gave me a little shove. "Good team, us."

16

Flat Island

A rescue truck arrived at the beach, lights swirling. A guy jumped out, grabbed a red float, and headed down into the water. "Someone's going to swim out to us," I said.

Clarence stood up and waved his arm back and forth. Then he held up a thumb. But the guy kept on swimming toward us.

"Why you doing that?" I asked. "Can any-one see us?"

"They got binoculars."

Clarence sat down, holding Willy against him. "How you doing, brah?" Willy nodded.

Clarence looked at the sky. "Storm moving on."

"Good," I said. "Enough bad weather for a while."

Clarence chuckled. "Keep rubbing his legs. Willy, talk to us. How you doing?"

Willy opened his eyes. "Okay," he whispered.

"Good. You going be fine. Help coming."

The chop on the ocean seemed to be dying down.

Willy dozed off for a second, then snapped his eyes open. They were red and squinty.

The guy with the float was almost halfway now.

Clarence raised his chin toward the skiff. "Those oars? If you didn't have those cables, the boy would be gone."

I cringed at how close I'd come to cutting them off!

"Smart, you."

"Ledward thought of it."

"Your mama's boyfriend?"

"Yeah. You know him?"

Clarence shook his head. "Only from Stella."

"What'd she say?"

He chuckled. "She said your house would fall apart if he stopped coming over."

"What?" I nearly choked. All Stella ever

did was complain about Ledward, except to say he cooked good. "Stella said that?"

Clarence nodded. "You and your family lucky. I know plenny houses falling apart."

I gaped at him. "You sure we're talking Stella?"

Clarence laughed. "Funny, you."

Stella had stood up for Ledward. Unbelievable.

But she was right. Ledward was always doing something around our house, including telling me how I should help out. Cut the grass. Do the dishes. Take the trash out. Clean the garage. Water the plants. "Your home is like your body," he said once. "You keep it good, it keeps you good."

Willy coughed and spat up some liquid.

Clarence rubbed his back. "You swallowed some dirty water, boy."

Willy nodded. "Tastes like dirt."

Clarence and I looked up when we heard the helicopter.

17

A Son with Courage

The rescue helicopter settled down on Flat Island. I covered my head. I'd never seen one so close. It was loud! Its rotors shot stinging sand in my face.

Streak cowered.

Two men jumped out and ran toward us. Their name tags said STEVENSON and HIRANO.

Hirano carried a white medical kit. He squatted to look at Willy.

"Anyone still in the water?" Stevenson shouted over the noise of the helicopter.

I pointed to the rescue swimmer. "Just that guy."

Stevenson signaled that everything was all right. The swimmer waved, turned, and headed back to shore.

"Everybody here!" Clarence shouted. "But Willy needs help!"

Stevenson and Hirano took Willy's temperature and checked him out. Hirano put everything back in the medical kit. "Temperature is down, but he seems okay. Probably swallowed a lot of water. Might be some bacteria that could make him sick."

Willy tried to struggle up.

"Hold on," Stevenson said. "We'll carry you."

Hirano jogged back to the helicopter.

"Is he going to be all right?" I asked.

"Sure," Stevenson said. "We just have to warm him up and check him out."

Hirano came back with a litter. They loaded Willy on it. Willy had enough left in him to grin.

I made a fist. "See you soon, bud."

"There's room for all of you," Stevenson said. "Even the dog."

Clarence turned toward the skiff. "We fine. We got to bring the boat back."

Stevenson looked at me. "That okay with you?"

I nodded. "It's not so stormy now."

"That was a wild one, wasn't it?"

"Crazy wild."

Stevenson and Hirano took Willy to the helicopter. They set him down inside and turned to wave.

Clarence and I watched them rise into the sky.

The pulsing sound faded as they flew back over the beach. Willy's parents headed up to their car.

"Where are they taking him?" I asked.

"Hospital, prob'ly. We'll find out."

We watched until we couldn't see them anymore.

For the first time I started thinking about Mom. How worried she must be . . . and how much trouble I would be in.

"Come!" Clarence said. "We go home."

We carried the boat to the water. Streak jumped aboard. I got in and sat with her in the bow. Clarence pushed off, set the oars in the oarlocks, and began to row through the choppy water.

Flat Island shrank behind us. Funny, I thought. I'd seen that island for years and had never been out to it. Never even thought much about it. But I loved it now. It had saved me and Willy . . . and Streak!

"What you going do when we get back?" Clarence asked over his shoulder.

"Get killed by Mom."

"Killed!" He laughed. "For what?"

"Scaring her."

Clarence rowed. The muscles in his back rippled. His tattooed shoulders spanned from one side of the skiff to the other. "Maybe you scared her," he said, "but she won't be angry."

"How do you know?"

"No mama going be angry at a son with courage."

"Courage? What if it was just stupid?"

"You call saving your friend stupid?"

"No, I meant–"

"You know what I going do?" Clarence said.

"What?"

"Go home. Take a hot shower. Eat."

I hugged Streak close. She'd stopped trembling.

Yep. Mom was going to kill me.

18

No Blood

Clarence maneuvered the skiff like an expert.

I looked over my shoulder at the beach. A small crowd was waiting: Mom, Stella, Darci, Clarence's cousin Rudy the cop, the rescue truck crew, the boys who'd watched me sail out to sea, and some other people.

"Hang on," Clarence said.

I turned back just as he dug the oars into the water and pulled hard, one, two, three times. Then, using the oars like rudders, we caught a wave and sailed in, all the way to the beach.

The bow thunked sand.

The crowd clapped and cheered.

The three boys ran up to grab the skiff.

Streak jumped out and ran up the beach. Clarence stowed the oars, and the two of us stepped out into the water.

Stella ran down and flung her arms around Clarence. "Whoa," he said. "I not going anywhere."

"I can't believe you did that!" Stella said.

"What? Catch a wave with the boat?"

"No, silly, swim out to get Calvin and Willy!"

Clarence waved that off. "Pfff. Anybody do that."

Mom and Darci crushed me with hugs as everyone crowded in around us.

Clarence put his big hand on my head. "This boy one hero."

I looked down. I sure didn't feel like a hero. I just felt tired.

Mom looked at me, her eyes shiny with tears.

What? Did I have blood on me or something? I rubbed my face and looked at my fingers. No blood.

"Mom?"

"Thank heaven you're safe," she whispered. "I've never been so scared in my life."

"I'm fine, Mom, I–"

"Shhh," she said. "Not now, Calvin. Just come home."

She pushed me away and looked at me. "How's Willy?"

"Fine, Mom. They took him in the helicopter. He swallowed a lot of water."

"Oh, no . . . not that filthy river water."

"Yeah."

She winced.

I turned toward my skiff. Clarence already had it figured out. "We carry um," he said. "You and me. Easy."

I looked back at Mom. She didn't want to leave me.

But she nodded, took Darci's hand, and walked back up the sand. "Come home right now."

"I will."

Rudy the cop came down and shook with Clarence, local style. "Howzit, cousin?"

Clarence flicked his eyebrows. "I wasn't speeding, Officer, promise."

Rudy humphed, then turned to me. "I thought I told you to stay home . . . or was I just talking to myself?"

I looked down.

Rudy said, "I let you off this time, kid, but next–"

"I didn't mean to. Really, I just–"

Rudy and Clarence laughed. "He only

joking," Clarence said, shoving me gently with his big hand. "Ne'mind him. We got a boat to carry."

Rudy smiled. "You two did good."

Stella looked at me. "Were you scared?"

Had I been?

"No," I said. "I didn't think about it."

But I prob'ly should have been, I thought. If you live near the ocean the first thing you'd better know is how to get out of trouble in the water. I was pretty good at it, but Willy sure wasn't.

"What you did was brave."

I couldn't believe it. Stella had said something nice to me.

Clarence clapped his hand on my shoulder. "The hero of Hawaii." He squeezed.

I looked up at Clarence. "I didn't even know you could swim like that. I mean, that was a long way out."

"He's a surfer," Stella said, kissing his cheek. "He does that all the time, don't you?"

Clarence shrugged. "You live Hawaii, you live the ocean, ah?"

"True," I said.

He tapped my arm. "The boat."

Stella hugged him again. She gave my shoulder a squeeze.

I stood gaping as she ran to catch up with Mom and Darci.

19

Absolute
Luckiest Mom

By the time we got the boat home and Clarence drove off, the raging storm had blown away from the islands. Maybe it fizzled out somewhere over the ocean. Except for what me and Willy had just been through, it was the best storm ever in my whole life so far.

But not for Mom.

"I don't want to see anything like that again for the rest of my life," she said later in the kitchen. "If I could just take a bath and lie on the couch with my magazines . . ."

She sighed.

I was starting to doze at the counter when Julio called. "I heard Willy almost drowned," he said.

I told him the story.

"Ho, man," he said. "So he's okay now?"

"Yeah, I guess. I've been trying to call him but no one answers."

"Wow."

"I'll call you when I know something."

"Yeah, good."

We hung up.

I sat around yawning and rubbing my eyes while Mom and Stella went for Chinese take-out. Darci was on the floor in the living room watching cartoons. She didn't seem to mind postponing her party.

I was asleep with my head on my arms when Mom and Stella came back.

"Wake up, sleepyhead," Mom said. "We got your favorite . . . beef tomato."

"Yeah . . . I'm awake."

Plink.

The leak bowl only had a little bit of water in it.

I looked up at the sagging ceiling.

"Ledward should be here any minute to look at that," Mom said. "The flooding is over, thank goodness. He's staying for dinner."

Plink.

"I'm calling Willy again." I took the phone into the dining room.

He was home!

"Hey," he said. "Just got back. What a day, huh?"

"You okay?"

He sneezed. "Thanks to you. That was scary."

"Very."

"I can hardly stay awake."

"Me too."

We let a few seconds of silence go by. I cringed, thinking about that wall of mud water at the end of the river. "Let's not do that again, okay?"

"Fine with me."

"Where'd that helicopter take you?"

"Somewhere like an airfield. Some guys checked me out, gave me some kind of pills and a cool space blanket. My parents came and got me." He paused. "Boy, were they shook up."

"Yeah, my mom, too."

We were silent again.

"You going to school tomorrow?" I asked.

"Sure. I'm fine. Just tired. But all I want to see when I wake up in the morning is the big old sun. Forget that rain."

"Like forever."

"Hey, how's Streak?"

"Asleep."

Willy laughed. "That's me in a few minutes. So, see you at school."

"Laters."

We hung up. I took the phone back in the kitchen.

"How is he?" Mom asked.

"Same old Willy."

"I hope so."

I looked at Mom. "What do you mean?"

"Well . . . sometimes a terrifying experience like that can affect us deep down inside. I just hope he doesn't end up afraid of the ocean."

"Afraid?"

"I'm not saying he will, Calvin. Just that it's possible."

That would be really bad, I thought. We lived on an island. The ocean was everywhere. It would be like being afraid of the air.

20

The Stop Sign

On my way out to feed Streak in the garage, I heard the quick tap of a horn. I looked up just as Ledward pulled into our driveway.

I filled Streak's bowl and headed out.

Ledward had put the canvas top up on his old army jeep. The tires and wheel wells were caked with mud.

"Howzit," he called.

"Hey."

Ledward got out and grabbed his tool box off the backseat. "Your mama told me you and your friend Willy had a big day."

"Big *scary* day."

Scarier for Willy, I thought. I hoped Mom was wrong about him being afraid of the water, like Darci was.

I shuddered. He could have drowned. Me and Streak, too.

Ledward nodded. "I was scared like that once."

"Really? You got caught in a river, too?"

"Not a river, no."

"Then what?"

He nodded toward the yard. "Let's sit."

We went out onto the grass. It was still wet, but who cared?

Ledward sat with his arms crossed over his knees. He looked out toward the mountains. "Well, let's see, I guess I was a couple years younger than you are now . . . eight or nine. I

went hunting with my pops. This was on the Big Island. You been on the Big Island?"

I shook my head. "Only this one."

"What? You never been off this island?"

"Nope."

Ledward scratched his head. "You and me got to take care of that, take a trip."

"Just us?"

"Man trip."

Cool!

"So what were you scared of?"

"The volcano."

I looked at him. "What's so scary about that?"

Everyone knew the volcano had been erupting for around thirty years. It was just part of life on the Big Island. All it did was make the sky smoky.

Ledward chuckled.

"Well, first, I was only a small kid, ah? But second, was the *power* of it. My pops took me down to see that end of the island. The volcano had flowed red hot down the hill toward one old village. Lucky thing they had scientists who study volcanoes, and they predicted the path, ah? So they warned the people and they all got out in time. But that lava came right down on top of their homes and covered them. Poof! The place was gone. All that was left was one stop sign. You go there now, you can still see it. Black lava rock everywhere . . . with that stop sign sticking out of it."

"Wow."

"To this day, I can still see it."

Why would that be so scary, I wondered? "Just the sign?"

He nodded. "Just the sign, but what it told me at that age was that against nature, you get what you get. Your only defense is to be ready. Not much more you can do."

He studied the river, still fat with muddy water. "Funny, yeah? That sign in my head all these years."

"Are you still scared of volcanoes?"

"Naah."

"Do you think Willy will be scared of the ocean now?"

Ledward turned to me. "Get him back in the water, soon as possible. You don't want him thinking about it too long."

I nodded. "Okay."

"He should learn some ways to get out of trouble."

For sure, I thought.

We sat in silence.

Ledward nudged me with his elbow. "Your mama said they calling you a hero."

"That was just Clarence fooling around." I wasn't any hero.

We sat watching the river.

"Ledward?"

"Yeah?"

"You know the cables you put on the oars?"

"So you wouldn't lose them."

"Yeah. Well . . . that was real smart. Willy might have . . . you know, drowned without them. So . . . so thank you."

"You're welcome."

Ledward tapped my knee and stood. "How's about you hero my tools into the house so we can take a look at that leak."

I couldn't help grinning as I picked up the tool box.

21

Great Riches

Ledward took a quick look at the leak before Mom called everyone to come eat. White Chinese take-out boxes were spread all around the table: beef tomato, beef broccoli, sweet-sour chicken, rice, wooden chopsticks, fortune cookies, and extra boxes of chicken chow mein. Darci's favorite meal.

I went straight to my fortune cookie: NOTH-ING IS EXACTLY AS IT SEEMS.

What kind of fortune was that?

Darci took a huge helping of chicken chow mein. She could eat all three boxes, if you let her.

"So, is our leak as bad as it looks?" Mom asked.

Ledward had cut the sagging part of the ceiling away so now you could look up through the hole and see the plywood roof.

"Small leak that made a big mess. I get it fixed up soon."

Mom put her hand on his. "Thank you, Led. You do so much for us."

"Naah," he said. "Just regular home main-tenance."

"Regular or not, we're lucky to have you around."

Ledward nudged a fortune cookie toward Mom. "Hey, check your fortune. See what it says."

Mom cracked it open and read it. "'Great riches are in your future.'"

Now, *that's* a fortune, I thought.

"I want that one," Stella said.

Mom gave it to her. "Take it. I already have great riches."

Huh? Where?

While we sat around eating Stella's cupcakes, which she had managed to make after all the excitement, Mom gave Darci a small gift-wrapped box.

"Happy birthday, sweetie."

Darci tore into it. "Oh, wow, Mom!"

"Stella and I picked it out for you."

Darci tilted the box toward me.

I peered in at a shiny silver bracelet. "Huh," I said.

Darci got up and hugged Mom and Stella.

What I'd gotten Darci at the Byodo-In Temple was good, and she'd love it . . . but it wasn't the *perfect* present. I needed time to find something that really meant something. "I'll give you my present next week at your party," I said.

Darci put the bracelet on and showed it to Ledward, who nodded. "That looks good on you."

Oh! I thought.

Yes!

An idea was coming to me.

I jiggled my leg. Yes! Yes!

If I could pull this off . . .

I couldn't sit at that table a second longer.

I went into the kitchen for the phone.

"Clarence," I said. "It's me, Calvin."

After dinner, Darci and I were lying on the living room floor watching TV. Mom was in the kitchen cleaning up, and Stella had disappeared into her bedroom.

Ledward was out in the dark backyard shoveling sand and dirt into the ditches the rain had made coming down off our roof in the storm. I could see him through the sliding screen door.

A mass of bugs swirled around the single patio light, bugs that would gladly eat me alive. But for some reason the bugs never bothered Ledward.

I tried to watch TV.

But I couldn't keep my thoughts from drifting back to the muddy ocean, remembering over and over how scared I'd been when I saw

Willy look at me just before he went under. It made me cringe.

Stop, stop, stop!

Think of . . . the temple! Yeah, and the giant golden Buddha . . . *Don't worry, be happy, everything's cool.*

"Darci," Mom called from the kitchen. "Turn the TV down!"

Darci picked up the remote and clicked off the TV. "What time is it?"

I peeked at the kitchen clock. "A little after seven."

"You think Willy's still up?"

"I don't know. Why?"

"Call him and see. I just thought of something."

22

Heroes

Mom liked Darci's idea.

"But can't it wait until morning, sweetie? It's dark out, and Willy needs sleep."

"But he's still up, Mom. Calvin said. And anyway, if I have to wait a week for my party, this is what I want to do for my real birthday."

My stubborn little sister. We grinned at each other.

Mom sighed. "Fine."

Darci ran and got some white paper, a pair of scissors, and a red crayon.

I sat watching her at the dining room table. "What are you doing?"

"You'll see."

Ledward came inside.

Stella peered out of her room.

Mom hooked her arm in Ledward's and we all watched Darci.

"There!" Darci said.

She'd made five white bands, which she taped around our right arms. She even made one for Streak that went around her belly. On each armband she'd drawn a red cross inside a circle.

"Perfect," she said, admiring her work.

But Stella was frowning. She looked at Mom. "Is there something weird in the dirt around here?"

We all looked at Stella, like . . . what?

"It really stinks in my room. I think the rain brought something up. It smells really bad."

"Huh," I said, giving her a thoughtful look.

Ah, doggy doody justice!

Stella gave me a squint back. "I had to close my window."

"That's funny," Mom said.

"Yeah," I said. "That is funny."

In the kitchen Darci got four of Stella's cupcakes, put them on a plate, and covered them with plastic wrap. "Let's go," she said, taking Stella's hand.

Mom and Ledward grinned at each other.

I brought up the rear with Streak, trying not to laugh when I thought of Stella's sour face. Justice!

Willy's mom answered the door.

"Wow," she said. "It's the Red Cross!"

"Is Willy here?" Darci asked.

"Come on in. He's in the living room."

"Willy!" Darci called. "We brought you cupcakes!"

That night I slept on the bottom bunk with Streak.

My thoughts and feelings were leaping around like fleas. And though Streak couldn't talk and help me figure it all out, it just felt good being with my dog.

I lay back with my hands behind my head.

Hero sounded good, but really, was I . . . a hero?

Maybe.

Kind of.

But I wasn't the only one.

Clarence was one, for sure. And Ledward, who'd fixed the oars and everything else. And Mom, who worked extra hard for us.

I reached down and scratched Streak's ears, smiling in the dark. "Hey, Streak," I said. "Is there something funny in the dirt around here?"

I laughed.

"You're a hero-dog."

Slept like a rock that night.

23

Darci's Famous Day

On Saturday a week later it was sunny hot. The river was back to its slow-moving, stinky self.

Anyone looking at our house must have thought there was going to be some kind of neighborhood carnival happening in our front yard.

It would be famous, all right. Kids were

going to come to Darci's party from all over the place. Only Clarence couldn't be there. He had to work.

But he stopped by to give Darci a leather necklace with a shark's tooth on it. "I coming back before your party's over, ah?"

He winked at me.

I nodded, hoping our timing would work out.

"Thanks, Clarence," Darci said, slipping the shark's tooth over her head. "I love it!"

Which reminded me that I still had to wrap what I'd gotten her at the temple.

While Ledward set up the slippery slide, I grabbed the color comics section from an old Sunday paper and quickly wrapped her present in my room. One of her presents, anyway.

No way I could wrap the other one.

Darci's slide was definitely the most amazing contraption our street had ever seen. The ramp was as tall as I was, which made the take-off part rocket fast.

Ledward set up the hose to squirt water down the tarps, keeping them slippery wet, and when someone asked, he'd send them down with a shove. Streak raced the shrieking sliders down the slope, barking her head off.

Down at the bottom of the yard Darci and her friends were pretending to be bowling pins, scattering and falling all over each other when someone came down the slide. Just beyond, the silent river moved toward the sea.

I was in line, waiting for my bazillionth run.

Maya stood shivering behind me, even though it was blazing hot. Julio and Willy were in front of me.

Julio's younger brothers Marcus, Diego, and Carlos had all shown up on tin can stilts. Julio pretended he didn't know them. His youngest brother, Cinco, was only three, so he was still at home.

Marcus and Diego were slippery sliding fools, but Carlos was afraid.

"*My mom gave me a nickel,*"
he sang as we stood in line.

"Go away!" Julio said. "Jeese!"

"*She said go buy a pickle.*"

"Not that song again." I covered my ears.

"I have an idea," Maya said, nudging me.
"Why don't you take him down the slide . . .
hold him on your lap."

I looked back at Maya. "Tell Julio. He's his
brother."

"Forget it," Julio said.

"But he likes *you*," Maya said. "Look, he's singing to you."

"I bought some bubble gum, a-chuka-chuka bubble gum."

Maya grinned. "It'll make him be quiet, I bet."

I snorted. But maybe it would work. "Hey, Carlos. You want to go down the slide with me?"

Carlos froze and looked up at the takeoff ramp. He shook his head.

"Come on," I said. "You can sit in my lap." I reached out.

Carlos turned to Julio.

"Don't look at me," Julio said. "I'm not taking you."

Carlos hesitated, then gripped my hand. Willy and Julio stepped aside to let us go by them in line. We climbed the ramp.

"Looks like you

got a new friend," Ledward said, holding the hose.

"He's a pest."

"Good luck!" Maya said.

I sat on the ramp. Ledward helped Carlos into my lap. "Ready?"

I nodded. "Do it!"

Boom! Ledward sent us off with a shove.

Carlos and I blasted down the slide, banging off the ramp onto the slippery blue tarps that zipped us toward the river. "Yee-haw!" I yelled.

Carlos's fingers dug into my arms.

We slid to a grassy stop at the bottom.

"Again! Again!" Carlos hopped out of my lap and grabbed my hand, tugging me up. "Again! Again! Again!"

Carlos went down on his own after that.

On his belly.

On his side.

Headfirst.

Feetfirst.

Upside down and backwards. That kid was unstoppable.

Julio couldn't believe it. "What did you do to him? You got some kind of magic, or what?"

I raised my arms and made muscles. "Incredible Hulk."

For the rest of the day Carlos stuck to me like a shadow . . . a nice shadow that didn't sing. Julio and Willy thought it was hilarious. But I didn't care. It was like having a little brother.

After around nine thousand times down the slide, Mom came over and put her hand on my shoulder. "We're going to have ice cream and cupcakes soon, and Darci's going to open her presents. Did you get something for her?"

"Yup."

Mom raised one eyebrow. "What is it?"

"It's good, Mom. You'll see."

24

Speechless

Mom, Ledward, Stella, and I watched as Darci opened her presents, surrounded by her friends. So far, she'd gotten a gift card for pizza; a T-shirt that said I DIDN'T DO IT... SERIOUSLY on it; two manga books, Yotsuba&! #1 and Naruto #27; a stuffed raccoon;

Chinese handcuffs; and a humongous Hershey bar.

"That slide was a great idea," Ledward whispered as Darci chose another present to open. "Everyone had a good time."

"I saw it on TV."

Ledward chuckled.

I heard a car drive up. Yes!

"Mom, look!" Darci called, holding up something wrapped in newspaper. "It's from Calvin!"

"That's just the small one," I said.

Mom turned to me. "The small one?"

I shrugged, suddenly worried that my idea was stupid. The small one she'd like . . . but the other one was kind of . . . different.

I heard the car door thump.

Darci ripped into the color comic paper.

"This I've got to see," Stella whispered.

"Calvin!" Darci shouted. "I love it! I love it!" She held it up.

A book.

Birds of Hawaii.

"Now you can name those birds," I said.

Darci got up, stepped over the crumpled wrapping paper, and hugged me.

"I got it at the temple."

Darci grabbed Stella's hand. "We have to go back! Call Clarence!"

"There's more, Darce," I said. "I got you two presents."

"Two?"

I dipped my chin toward the front door as Clarence walked in wearing swimming shorts, a T-shirt, and rubber slippers.

"You got me *Clarence* for a present?"

"Yup."

Stella was as surprised as Darci.

Clarence gave Darci a big smile. "I going teach you how for be the best swimmer in this town. Won't be anything you can't do in the water. Calvin's idea."

Mom put a hand to her mouth, then grabbed my arm and pulled me close.

Darci looked at Clarence, then at me, then back at Clarence. Speechless for the first time in her life.

Clarence winked. "Start today, if you like."

"You can invite Willy, too, Darce," I added. "It's okay with Clarence."

Darci smiled, big. She reached out to shake Clarence's hand. "Deal," she said.

Clarence nodded. "You got it."

"After all, Darce," I said. "You live Hawaii, you live the ocean, ah?"

Mom surrounded me with her arms and whispered, "I'm so proud of you."

"I try, Mom. I try."

A Hawaii Fact:

In September 1992, Hurricane Iniki, whose name means "strong and piercing wind," became the most powerful hurricane to strike the Hawaiian Islands in recorded history. Damage was greatest on the island of Kauai, where over 1,400 houses were destroyed and more than 5,000 severely damaged. Steven Spielberg and his crew, who were preparing for the final day of on-location filming of the movie *Jurassic Park*, had to wait out the storm in a hotel.

A Calvin Fact:

You can listen to thunder after lightning and tell how close you came to getting hit. If you don't hear it, you got hit, so never mind.

 **Graham Salisbury** is the author of four other Calvin Coconut books: *Trouble Magnet, The Zippy Fix, Dog Heaven,* and *Zoo Breath,* as well as several novels for older readers, including the award-winning *Lord of the Deep, Blue Skin of the Sea, Under the Blood-Red Sun, Eyes of the Emperor, House of the Red Fish,* and *Night of the Howling Dogs.* Graham Salisbury grew up in Hawaii. Calvin Coconut and his friends attend the same school Graham did–Kailua Elementary School. Graham now lives in Portland, Oregon, with his family. Visit him on the Web at grahamsalisbury.com.

 **Jacqueline Rogers** has illustrated more than ninety books for young readers over the past twenty years. She studied illustration at the Rhode Island School of Design. You can visit her at jacquelinerogers.com.